John and the River Monster

First published 2007
Evans Brothers Limited
2A Portman Mansions
Chiltern Street
London W1U 6NR

Text copyright © Evans Brothers Ltd 2007
© in the illustrations Ian Benfold Haywood 2007

British Library Cataloguing in Publication Data

Harrison, Paul, 1969-
    John and the river monster. - (Spirals)
    1. Children's stories
    I. Title
    823.9'2[J]

ISBN-10: 0 237 53350 2 (hb)
ISBN-13: 978 0 237 53350 2 (hb)

ISBN-10: 0 237 53344 8 (pb)
ISBN-13: 978 0 237 53344 1 (pb)

Printed in China

Series Editor: Nick Turpin
Design: Robert Walster
Production: Jenny Mulvanny

John and the River Monster

Paul Harrison and
Ian Benfold Haywood

Long ago there was a quiet river valley,
where many people lived. In the
evenings they told old stories about a
terrifying beast that once lived deep in
the river. No one had ever seen it, apart
from one old woman, who said she'd
seen it when she was a girl, but
everyone thought she was mad.

In the village lived a boy called John, who was always in trouble. One day, while he was fishing, he caught the strangest, ugliest-looking wormy thing he'd ever seen.

"Yuck!" said John, and threw it back.

He went home and told his parents
what he had found. They remembered
the old stories and became very worried.
They told John not to mention what
had happened to anyone.

Soon he had forgotten all about it.

But down in the river the worm was growing. It grew great, big teeth in its great, big mouth; and it got hungrier and hungrier. One day it came out of the river looking for something to eat.

At first the worm would come out of
the river and gobble up sheep –
MUNCH, CRUNCH!

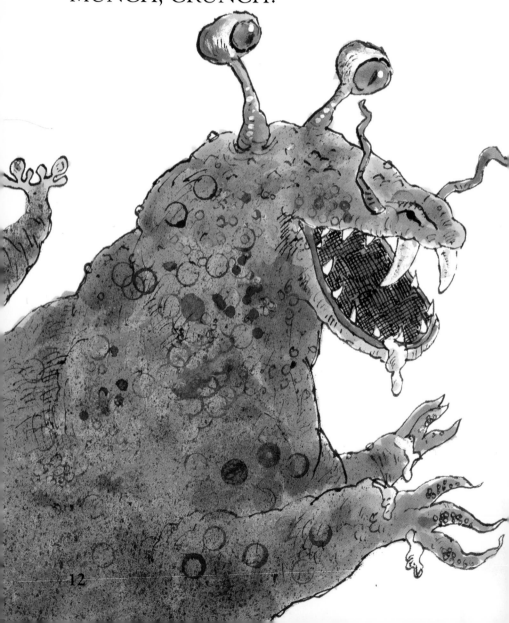

The local people were terrified. What would happen when they ran out of sheep?

They sent for brave knights to kill the worm.

However, the monster just wrapped the knights in its coils and squeezed until they popped. Soon the villagers were running out of both sheep AND knights.

Then the old woman came down from the hills.

"So there's a river monster is there?" she asked.

"Yes," the villagers replied, embarrassed about laughing at her before.

"Does it come
onto the land
and eat sheep?"
she asked.

"Yes," they
replied.

"Then someone here must have caught it once before and taken it from the river. Only they can kill it!" said the old woman.

John felt ashamed.

"It was me," he said. "But how can I kill it? It's already killed the knights. All I do is fish."

"You've caught it once, you can do it again," replied the woman.

The old woman took John to the
local blacksmith.

"John needs a sword and a special
suit of armour," she said.

The next day, the armour was ready.
All over it were sharp, metal spikes.
John put it on and waited by the river
for the beast, just as the old woman
had told him to.

Out it came gnashing its
terrible teeth.

The monster wrapped itself around
John, and began to squeeze tight.

But the spikes on the armour dug
into the monster's flesh, which made
it loosen its grip.

"I see you got the point," said John and, quick as a flash, lopped off the monster's head, which fell into the river with a plop.

The people rushed cheering to the
river and carried their new hero home
on their shoulders – once John had
taken his armour off, of course.

Why not try reading a Spirals book?

Megan's Tick Tock Rocket by Andrew Fusek Peters,
Polly Peters, and Simona Dimitri
ISBN 978 0237 53342 7

Growl! by Vivian French and Tim Archbold
ISBN 978 0237 53345 8

John and the River Monster by Paul Harrison and Ian
Benfold Haywood
ISBN 978 0237 53344 1

Froggy Went a Hopping by Alan Durant and Sue Mason
ISBN 978 0237 53346 5